HAND OF FATE

HAND OF FATE

DOTTI ENDERLE

2004
Llewellyn Publications
St. Paul, Minnesota 55164-0383, U.S.A.

Hand of Fate © 2004 by Dotti Enderle. All rights reserved. No part of this book may be used or reproduced in any manner whatsoever, including Internet usage, without written permission from Llewellyn Publications except in the case of brief quotations embodied in critical articles and reviews.

FIRST EDITION
First printing, 2004

Book design and editing by Kimberly Nightingale
Cover design by Kevin R. Brown
Cover illustration and interior illustrations © 2004 by Matthew Archambault

Library of Congress Cataloging-in-Publication Data
Enderle, Dotti, 1954–
Hand of fate / by Dotti Enderle
p. cm. –(Fortune Tellers Club ; 5)
Summary: After Anne is injured in an unusual accident, she misses cheer camp and a cheerleading award but, with the help of her Fortune Tellers' Club friends, is led to uncover a secret from her past.
ISBN 0-7387-0390-7
[1. Supernatural–Fiction. 2. Fate and fatalism–Fiction. 3. Adoption–Fiction. 4. Clubs–Fiction.] I. Title.

PZ7.E6964Han 2004
[Fic]–dc22

2003058740

Llewellyn Worldwide does not participate in, endorse, or have any authority or responsibility concerning private business transactions between our authors and the public.

All mail addressed to the author is forwarded but the publisher cannot, unless specifically instructed by the author, give out an address or phone number.

Any Internet references contained in this work are current at publication time, but the publisher cannot guarantee that a specific location will continue to be maintained. Please refer to the publisher's website for links to authors' websites and other sources.

Llewellyn Publications
A Division of Llewellyn Worldwide, Ltd.
P.O. Box 64383, Dept. 0-7387-0390-7
St. Paul, MN 55164-0383, U.S.A.
www.llewellyn.com

Printed in the United States of America

Other Books by Dotti Enderle

The Lost Girl

Playing with Fire

The Magic Shades

Secrets of Lost Arrow

Contents

CHAPTER 1 Crash! . . . 1

CHAPTER 2 Who's in Control? . . . 9

CHAPTER 3 Hand of Fate . . . 17

CHAPTER 4 Fate Happens . . . 25

CHAPTER 5 Looking for Answers . . . 33

CHAPTER 6 The Why Factor . . . 41

CHAPTER 7 The Séance . . . 49

CHAPTER 8 Fate's Door . . . 61

CHAPTER 9 Alice's Wonderland . . . 71

CHAPTER 10 It's in the Stars . . . 83

CHAPTER 11 Living a Lie . . . 91

CHAPTER 12 Fate Revealed . . . 99

CHAPTER 13 Visiting the Past . . . 105

CHAPTER 14 The Missing Puzzle Piece . . . 113

CHAPTER 1

Crash!

Cheerleader of the Year. Anne could visualize the beautiful trophy. The weight and feel of it. The applause during the ceremony. It was hers, no doubt. She stood near the street corner, gazing down the road at the line of cars. The roaring of engines was a reminder of her excitement. Her motor raced too. She turned to Beth Wilson, standing next to her. "What time is it now?"

"Two minutes since the last time you asked. Relax. We're early. And besides, my sister is never late for anything. Especially this."

As another minute passed, Anne's stomach tied itself into a few more knots. She couldn't wait to get to the weekend cheer camp. This was the weekend they'd announce Avery Cheerleader of the Year, and Anne was going to be the school's only seventh grader to ever take home that award. She was sure of it. Of course, the hints from the other girls on the team assured her even more.

She looked at her watch. "It's 4:37."

Beth giggled. "Jill has been a cheer counselor for two years now. She's not going to be late. She said she'd pick us up at 4:45, remember? I can't believe you're making such a big deal over this Cheerleader of the Year thing." Her tone reeked of jealousy.

Anne bounced in place, antsy and anxious. Why couldn't Jill be early this time? Anne wanted to get to camp and get this fantastic weekend started. But what if Beth and her sister had devised a plot to keep her from going? That would certainly give Beth a better chance to win the award. That was silly, thinking like that. She had to get a hold of herself and stop worrying.

"There she is," Beth said, pointing across the highway. Jill sat three cars back at the intersection, waiting for the light to turn green. "Jill!" Beth yelled, waving her arms and running several yards away to get Jill's attention.

Anne felt a lift of relief. She crossed her arms and swayed back and forth, full of energy. She wished they could just run across the street, hop into Jill's car, and finally be on their way. But for safety's sake, she stayed well back from the road.

Traffic had slowed to a crawl as a long train of cars crept by with their headlights on. Anne watched as a cop zoomed around them, the sun glinting off the polished chrome of his motorcycle. He motioned the cars to continue on through the red light. That's when Anne realized that it was a funeral procession. A slow ... turtle-crawling ... snail-inching ... funeral procession. Jill was caught on the other side. Darn! It could be another fifteen minutes or more before she crossed the intersection.

Anne figured whoever had died must have been one popular fellow. The headlights stretched as far into the distance as she could see. *Come on, come on! Do they have to drive so slow?* The light changed again, and she looked down at her watch. 4:42. Check-in time at the camp was 7:00, and it would take at least two hours to get there. She stood, bouncing up and down on her toes, as though that would get the traffic moving more quickly. Counting cars didn't help either. The light changed again.

Beth stood some distance away making hand signals to her sister. Anne wished they'd waited across the street to begin with. That would have made things much easier, but there was no pavement on the other side.

A pale blue car rolled slowly to the red light and proceeded through. Anne turned toward Beth, who was still smiling and yakking in some weird sign language. At least Beth was smiling. Anne refused to smile until she was on her way. And she was saving her biggest smile for the Cheerleader of the Year ceremony.

As Anne turned back, she saw a white pickup truck approaching from the other direction. The man looked as though he had no intention of slowing down. The traffic light was green on his side, after all. Anne didn't see the motorcycle cop anywhere around. The pickup raced faster, the man obviously in as big a hurry as she was. He must have been concentrating on the green light rather than the traffic. The blue car was still proceeding through when the pickup crashed into it, creating a horrific sound of crunching metal and breaking glass. The pickup bounced off the car, flew backward, and was rolling . . . rolling . . . right toward Anne!

She dove out of the way, feeling the wind from the pickup sweep by her. Dirt and debris rolled with it. She hit the pavement hard, wondering for a moment if she'd been struck by the truck. Anne cowered briefly, shielding her head. The vehicle had just missed her, but only by inches.

She lay on the ground, her head buried. She peeked up to see a panicked crowd of people hitting their brakes, hopping out of cars, and hurrying to help the drivers and passengers. Beth's unnecessary screams were the loudest.

A woman and a teenage boy rushed over to Anne. "Are you hurt?" the lady asked.

Anne recognized the boy—Troy Messina. He and Anne had been in school together since second grade, and he'd made it obvious ever since then that he had a major crush on her.

Anne felt like she'd been knocked down. She sat up and examined a large scrape on her elbow. Other than some dirt in her left eye, she felt okay. "I'm all right."

She'd fallen on her right side, which had taken the worst of it. Her Avery Wildcat t-shirt looked like it had been used to clean a gutter. And her arm and leg were both covered in black grime.

"Well, okay then," said Mrs. Messina, her face looking unsure. "Come on, Troy. Let's see if anyone needs some assistance." She hurried away to the crowd gathered at the pickup. Troy hesitated.

"Let me help you up, Anne." He fidgeted a little, then extended his hand.

Beth knelt down next to Anne. "I'll take care of her."

Troy scratched his head. He looked like he wanted to speak, but the words were trapped in his throat. He nodded, and jogged away to where his mother stood.

"Were you hit?" Beth asked, her voice trembling. Anne noticed the tears streaking her face. She shook her head no.

Beth let out a huge sigh. "You just sit and rest a moment, Anne. The good news is that traffic is stopped. Jill can cross over now."

Anne laughed at that. "Good news? Traffic will be stopped here forever."

She felt some relief when she looked over her shoulder and saw some people helping the man in the pickup. He came out with barely a scratch. The people in the blue car seemed fine too.

Beth nudged Anne. "We could walk over to Jill's car. I bet she can turn around and find a different route."

"All right," she said to Beth. "Unless they need me here as a witness or something."

Beth jerked her head up as though scanning the crowd. "I'd say they have plenty of witnesses!" She pulled Anne's arm to get her on her feet.

Anne tried to stand, but the moment she put her weight on her left foot, a hot flame of pain shot through her calf. "Ow!" She collapsed.

"What is it?" Beth asked, looking her over.

"I don't know." She tried to stand again, but it was like someone held a lit match to her leg.

"Come on. We need to hurry."

Anne tried again. The searing pain pierced her.

"What's wrong?"

"I don't know," Anne said, suddenly feeling panicked. "I can't stand up!"

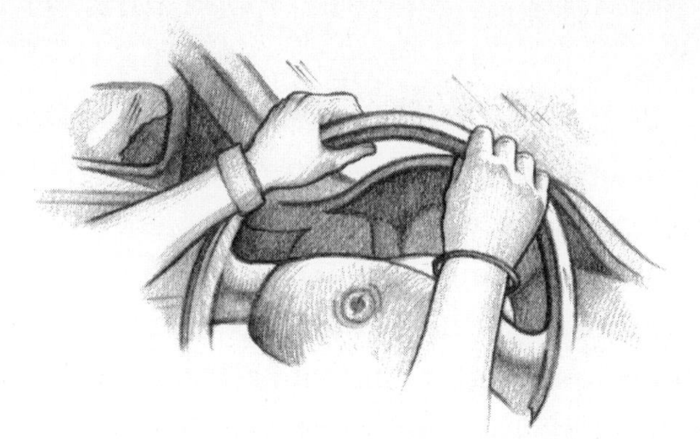

CHAPTER 2

Who's in Control?

The street corner soon looked like a parking lot with red flashing lights blinking everywhere. Anne's worries were lifted when she saw her father's car cutting through the drive near the shopping center. He parked away from the ambulances and wrecker trucks, and hurried toward her. His smoky gray hair offset his worried face. Anne reached out for him.

"What's wrong?" he asked.

"I don't know. I can't stand on my left leg at all."

Beth ran her hand down Anne's leg. "Mr. Donovan, a paramedic checked, and she couldn't find any cuts or blood."

"Do you think it's broken?" he asked.

Anne shook her head. She couldn't feel any thing broken. But it might be. It hurt like crazy every time she touched it *here*—she pointed to her calf.

Dad scooped her up into his arms, and she clung tightly to his neck, inhaling the faint scent of Old Spice. The paramedic walked over, clip board in hand. "Are you her grandfather?"

"No. I'm her father."

"She needs that leg x-rayed," the paramedic said. "Do you want us to take her in the ambulance?"

"No need," he answered. " I'll drive her to the emergency room myself. Thanks anyway."

Just then a car horn blasted through the commotion. Jill crept along the shoulder of the road, in line with the rest of the traffic trying to bypass the wreck. She was motioning frantically toward them.

Beth looked at Anne, her face apologetic. "I . . . I . . ."

"Go on," Anne said. "No reason for you to miss the camp." Realization set in. Beth would go, but what about her? Could she catch up later?

Beth gave her a guilty smile, and ran toward Jill's car, her cheer bag flopping against her.

Anne's dad carefully set Anne in the backseat, and again zigzagged through the shopping center parking lot into the street.

* * *

"It's the darndest thing," Doctor Cannon said. He slipped the x-ray on the light box for them to see. "There's a tiny hair-thin piece of wire in her leg."

Anne looked at the copper-colored wire, coiled like a glowing worm under her skin, "How did it get there? There's no hole or cut?"

"This wire is so thin, I'm guessing the force of the debris kicked up by the truck sent it into your skin so quickly, it shot through without a mark. I've seen this type of thing before, though it's rare."

Anne's dad rubbed his brow. "How are you going to remove it?"

"Surgically. But it's a minor procedure. She can go home afterward. She'll need crutches for a few days."

Suddenly the permanence of the situation sank in. No cheer camp. No award. Anne felt like crying. She closed her eyes and saw the truck rolling at her.

The divider curtain opened and Juniper peeked in. "Phew!" she sighed.

Gena followed Juniper to the examining table. "We heard your leg was crushed in a five-car pileup."

Mr. Donovan chuckled. "From my wife, no doubt. I better give her a call and tell her we'll be home later."

Anne could feel the tears stinging her eyes. "I won't be going to cheer camp."

"Great!" Gena said. "Fate stepped in and spared you a weekend with Snotty Twin Number One."

"Fate?" Anne sneered, wondering what she'd done to deserve this. "I was going to be the first seventh grader to win Cheerleader of the Year." The tears rolled uncontrollably.

"It's okay," Juniper said, touching her arm, "Everything happens for a reason. Maybe something good will come out of this."

"Surgery?" Anne wiped her tears, refusing to listen to any news about the bright side.

Gena shrugged. "I'm with Juniper on this one. Everything happens for a reason."

"Well, when you find the reason for this, would you please report back to me?" Anne spat. "Because I don't think this is going to amount to anything but a sore leg and a lost weekend!"

"Relax," Juniper said. "It's no one's fault."

Anne considered this. *Yes, it is. It's someone's fault.*

The doctor pushed back in, followed by Rachael, the nurse who dates Gena's father. "Sorry, ladies," the doctor said. "It's time to do a little surgery. We need you to clear out."

"I don't know," Rachael said. "I think Gena likes blood and guts."

Gena rolled her eyes. "Oh yeah. Save some for me, okay?"

"I'll call you tomorrow," Juniper said to Anne, as she and Gena disappeared behind the curtain. Anne could hear their mumbling slowly fade.

"You're shivering. Would you like a blanket?" Rachael asked.

"I'd rather have a Cheerleader of the Year jacket."

"What?" Rachael looked puzzled.

"Nothing," Anne said, all hope fizzling away. The overwhelming smell of alcohol was bad enough, but when Rachael brought out a needle, Anne shivered even more. "Yes. I want a blanket . . . and a blindfold . . . and lots of stuff to numb the pain."

Rachael giggled. "You won't feel the surgery."

"No, the numbing stuff is for the needle," Anne said, cringing. She'd rather fall from the top of her cheer squad's pyramid than get a shot any day!

When Rachael unwrapped a warm blanket and laid it across her, Anne's thoughts went back to fate. Fate. Who decides fate? Who's *really* in control? Who's fault was this? She played the scene over in her mind—the funeral procession rolling through the red light—the truck gaining speed to clear the green light. The crashing, the rolling, the crunching, the debris, the panic. It was certainly someone's fault. The driver of the pickup? The driver of the blue car? The motorcycle cop for not being there?

Anne's mind was too occupied to feel the needle injection or even the surgery. She refused to believe she was just in the wrong place at the wrong time. Several "what ifs" drifted through her thoughts, but she kept returning to the question of whose fault it was that she was lying on this hospital table instead of a cot at cheer camp.

If only that stupid funeral hadn't been in the way. That thought sparked another, "If only . . ."

Who's fault was it? If whoever was riding in that hearse hadn't died, she wouldn't be here right now. *If only.* Anne was convinced. *It's his fault. The person who died. He did this to me!*

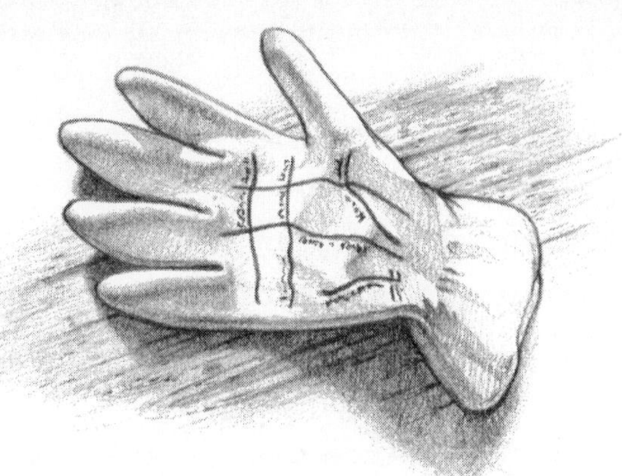

CHAPTER 3

Hand of Fate

The phone rang late the next morning, pulling Anne out of a deep and weary sleep. Her mind was groggy, making the events of yesterday seem more like a dream than a memory. But the ache in her left leg kicked her back into reality. She pulled the covers off and examined the large bandage taped to her leg. The skin around it looked scarlet-purple, like a nasty zit ready for popping. The muscles felt knotted, and she wondered if her left leg wasn't two inches shorter now than her right. *Silly,* she thought. But what about her famous toe-touches? The ones that earned her the title Cheerleader of the Year? That sparked a new reality. It wouldn't be her title this year. It was like everything had forcefully been flushed out of her.

Anne limped into the kitchen, where her mother sat, mending a skirt by the light of the window.

"How do you feel this morning?"

Stiff-legged, Anne plopped down in a chair and flopped forward on the table, burying her head in her arms. She didn't feel like talking.

"Would you like some breakfast?"

She peeked a blurry eye at her mom. "No."

Mom kept stitching. After a moment of dead silence she said, "Anne, I know you're upset. I'd be upset too. But this is a small price to pay considering what could have happened. We're so blessed that you're still in one piece."

Anne thought about what could have happened if she hadn't jumped out of the way. "Yeah, I know. Fate." She said it, but was still unmoved by the words. What if she hadn't jumped out of the way? Would hers have been the next funeral procession?

Could she have caused a chain of events that could screw up someone else's weekend, and cost them something important? "Mom, did you throw out the old newspapers?"

"No, they're still in the recycle bin."

Anne hobbled to the door leading out to the garage. There was probably a week's worth of newspapers out there, and each one had an obituary section. She was determined to find out who did this to her. As she headed back through the kitchen with an armful of papers, her mom said, "That was Juniper on the phone. She and Gena will be over later."

* * *

When Juniper and Gena arrived, Anne was still in her pajamas sitting on the bed, her leg propped on a teddy bear. Her fingertips were gray from newspaper ink.

"We came to cheer you up," Juniper said, holding a wrapped present in her hand.

"Don't say the word *cheer,*" Anne snapped.

Gena scooted some scattered newspapers over and hopped onto the bed. "Well, it looks like someone woke up on the wrong side of the surgical table."

Anne's bitterness had the best of her, and she refused to give in to Gena's jokes. She kept thumbing through the papers, ignoring her.

Juniper crept over, cradling the gift like it was an ancient relic from King Tut's tomb. "You're upset."

"Yeah," Gena said, holding up a section with obituaries. "Not exactly the funny papers. Who died?"

Anne snatched it out of her hand. "You will if you don't stop acting like a jerk."

Gena's face sunk for a moment, then she smiled. "Well, we came to cheer you up. Looks like our job is done. Let's go, Juniper."

Gena started to get up, but Juniper cut in. "Anne, we know you got skunked on this deal, but don't take it out on us. Especially after we brought you a present."

She shoved the gift at Anne, forcing her to take it.

Anne's sourness melted, and she couldn't control her tears. "I know I shouldn't be mad. It seems so selfish. But I can't help it. This was going to be *my* weekend. Why me?" Her last words were drowned in sobs. She didn't think she'd ever understand it. How could life play such a cruel trick?

"Open the gift," Juniper said, once Anne had wiped her nose. "We made it ourselves."

Anne tore into the package. Inside the box was a latex glove filled with birdseed. Using colored markers, Juniper and Gena had marked the lines of the palm and fingers, and labeled each one like a road map. "This isn't like palmistry, is it?"

"Nope," Gena said. "It's a Hand of Fate."

Anne liked the squishy feel of it. "A Hand of Fate?"

"Yeah," Juniper said. "We made it up. You take a coin, ask a question, and flip it up and onto the hand. Whichever line it lands on is the answer."

Anne suddenly felt lifted. The only thing she loved as much as cheerleading was being a member of the Fortune Tellers Club. "Let's try it right now."

Gena dug a dime out of her jeans pocket, and handed it to Anne. "What are you going to ask?"

Anne kicked with her right leg, knocking all the newspapers off onto the floor except for two pages. Each held the obituary of someone who'd passed away earlier in the week, and whose funeral was held yesterday. She'd narrowed it down to three people.

She looked at the write-up for George O'Hara, age eighty-two. Anne closed her eyes and tried to picture this man in her mind. She flipped the coin. It landed on the bed about a foot away from the hand. Nope, not George O'Hara.

"Can you let us in on this too?" Juniper asked. "What do you want to know about these dead people?"

"I want to know why they died," she said quickly, looking at the next obituary.

"You don't need the Hand of Fate for that!" Gena said, twirling the page around toward her. "It says right here . . . uh . . . Alice Lang, age 32.

Died of complications after a long battle with cancer."

"I don't want to know *how* they died. I want to know *why* they died and had to be on *that* street at *that* moment. But first, I have to figure out who's funeral it was."

Anne closed her eyes and tried to picture Alice Lang. Only thirty-two. She flipped the coin and it came down right into the palm of the Hand of Fate. The line on the hand read, *Fate will reveal something important soon.*

"It's her," Anne said. "Alice Lang. It's all her fault!"

CHAPTER 4

Fate Happens

Gena leaned over and looked into Anne's ear.

"What are you doing?" Anne asked, swatting her away.

"Are you sure a wire didn't get stuck in your brain too?"

"Look, I know it's weird," Anne said, "but it's true! If this woman hadn't died, I would be Cheerleader of the Year!"

"You don't know for sure it's her," Juniper argued.

Anne looked at Juniper with new tears stinging her eyes. "I know it. I know it. I just know it."

Gena sat back down on the bed. "Okay, so it's her. What are you going to do . . . beat her up?" She picked up the obituary and waved it toward Anne. "Seems to me the poor lady's been punished enough."

It didn't even seem like revenge anymore. It was curiosity. A curiosity that gnawed at her. She picked up the Hand of Fate and nervously squished the fingers. Her mind raced for a solution. "I need a phone book."

"I don't think she's going to answer," Gena said.

"I need to get the phone book."

"Why?" Juniper asked. Her face looked genuinely troubled.

"You'll see," Anne said, hopping up and hobbling out of her bedroom. She limped to the corner desk in the living room, grabbed the Yellow Pages, and limped back to her room. "What's the name of the funeral home listed in the paper?"

Gena crumpled the paper and dramatically jabbed it to her chest. "Omigosh! You're seriously going to do it! You're going to dig this woman up and beat her to a pulp!"

"Just give me the name of the funeral home," Anne said, rolling her eyes.

Just then the phone rang. The girls turned toward Anne's kitty-cat phone sitting on the dresser across the room.

Gena rested her chin on her knees. "Anne, you're the only person I know who has a phone that meows."

On the fourth meow, Juniper hurried over and picked it up. "Donovan residence."

Anne watched as Juniper's face steeled like armor. "Who is *this?*" she asked, obviously repeating the caller's sarcastic greeting. Of course, Anne didn't have to ask Juniper who it was. Juniper would only take that tone with one of the Snotty Twins.

"Hi, Beth," Anne said.

Gena made some gagging noises and grabbed her throat. Anne turned away so she could hear Beth.

"I just wanted to check up on you," Beth said, her voice sounding distant in the hum of the receiver.

"I'm fine," Anne lied. "How's camp?"

Beth burst into excitement. "It's so much fun! They've brought in this really cool guy cheerleader from the university. He showed us some hard stunts, but we did them. We looked awesome. I really think we're the best middle school team here!"

Every word clawed deeper into Anne's heart. Her jealousy now felt like a large green elephant sitting on her chest. "That's great," she said with effort.

"I wish you were here! We're having some fun contests too. Susan won the 'short stuff' award for being the shortest cheerleader at camp. Anne, I know you would have won the 'vertical' award for being the tallest. And the door prizes are awesome! This morning I won a complete make-up kit to use for competitions. And . . ."

Anne couldn't listen anymore. The only sound she heard was her own voice shouting in her mind. *Alice Lang, why? Why did you do this to me?*

"Well, I gotta go," Beth said suddenly. "Do you want to see if someone can drive you out here to watch the awards ceremony tomorrow night?"

"What?" Anne was stunned by that question.

"The awards? Don't you want to know who makes Cheerleader of the Year?"

Not anymore! "I can't," she said. "But you can fill me in on Tuesday."

"See ya!" Beth hung up the phone before Anne could even say goodbye. The green elephant got up, leaving her feeling flat and empty.

"What's the name of the funeral home?" Anne asked again.

Gena looked at Juniper as though asking permission to say it, then with a sigh, "Jacob Brothers."

Anne ran her finger down the page. She switched the phone back on and heard the kitty-cat purring a dial tone.

On the first ring the soft voice of a woman spoke. "Jacob Brother's Funeral Services. How may I help you?"

Anne stumbled for the right words. "Uh—yesterday you had a funeral. There was a car wreck. What I need to know is—"

"I'm sorry," the woman said, cutting Anne off. "I'm not at liberty to give out any information, however, I can give you the phone number of our attorney. He can answer any of your questions."

"Never mind," Anne said. She placed the phone back in its cradle.

"What?" Juniper blurted.

Anne shrugged. "I guess she thinks I'm suing them or something. She wouldn't talk."

"Well, that was certainly a *dead* end," Gena said. "But then it is a funeral home."

Juniper giggled a little. "I don't get it, Anne. You haven't told us what you're planning to do."

"I'm planning to find out about Alice Lang. Who she was. Where she lived. What she did. Why she died, and where she's buried."

"And what will that prove?" Juniper asked.

Anne considered the question. "It'll prove that I'm right." She held her left leg up and bent it at the knee. "It hurts when I put weight on my left foot, but I think I can pedal with my right foot, once I get going."

"We're going somewhere?" Gena asked.

"Yep," Anne said, taking some clothes from her closet. "We're going to pay a visit to Troy Messina."

"Do you like him?" Gena asked.

Anne painstakingly slipped on a pair of jeans and zipped them up. "I do today. He was at Alice's funeral. He has some important information for me."

"Why didn't you just ask him to begin with?" Juniper asked. "Wouldn't that have been easier than digging through the newspapers?"

Anne smiled, not wanting to admit that the thought hadn't really occurred to her. "Yes. That would have been easier. But then I wouldn't have gotten a chance to use my Hand of Fate. At least we know it works."

Anne propped her left foot up while Juniper tied her sneaker for her. She left her mom a note, and they headed out to their bikes.

"Go slow," Anne said, trying to get the feel of pedaling with one foot.

They rode out of the driveway and down the road. Anne felt each rotation of the bicycle's wheels bringing her closer and closer to her answers.

CHAPTER 5

Looking for Answers

Anne tried to keep her mind on other things as she pedaled. Her left leg was throbbing, mostly from being stretched out. It felt heavy and stiff. She knew she should have stayed put, keeping it propped up.

Her emotions were whirling chocolate in a blender. What was she doing? What did she really expect to find? Going to Troy's house might make him think she liked him. She didn't want to do that. Especially since she knew he had a major crush on her. And what about the note she'd left her mom? *We're going riding to exercise my leg.* Okay, she couldn't tell Mom she was going to see a boy, even though there was nothing to it. But Mom was too old-fashioned to understand that. And she definitely couldn't tell her why she really wanted to see Troy. That led to more mixed feelings. Was missing out on Cheerleader of the Year really this important? There was always next year. They arrived at Troy's before she could sort through all the jumble in her brain.

Gena and Juniper hitched their kickstands and headed for the door. Anne still stood on her bike, leaning to the right. What *was* she doing?

"Okay," Gena said, motioning Anne up. "This isn't carhop service. You'll have to ring the doorbell."

Juniper raised an eyebrow. "Changed your mind?"

Anne wasn't sure.

Gena headed back toward her bike. "I vote we forget all this and go back to consult the Hand of Fate. I need to know if my dad is going to have a seizure when he sees the grade I made on Thursday's math exam."

Anne ignored her and got off her bike. She felt like a puppet, pulled by strings. She rang the doorbell before she could change her mind. Troy answered.

"Hey! Uh, Anne. Are you feeling okay?"

Not really. "I'm fine," she answered, smiling shyly. "I just came to ask you some questions."

He shrugged. "Sure."

Anne paused, carefully working out how to ask. Before she could say a word, Gena popped off. "Who died?" Now Anne wished she'd come alone.

Troy looked at Gena, his eyes narrowed. Suddenly his face lit. "Oh, the funeral. That was a lady named Alice."

"How did you know her?" Anne asked. Troy scratched his head. "I didn't."

"You went to a funeral for someone you didn't know?" Juniper asked.

"My mom knew her."

Anne took an anxious step forward, trying not to put extra weight on her leg. "Is your mom here?"

Troy scratched his armpit this time. "No." Anne sighed. She wanted to forget the whole thing, go home, and lie down. But that puppet string tugged even harder. "Was she a good friend of your mom's?"

Troy rubbed his forehead. Anne couldn't help but think he was the fidgetiest person she'd ever seen. "Mom didn't really know her."

"Ahhhhhhh!" Gena's scream startled Anne. Troy and Juniper jumped too. "Troy! You just said your mom knew her. Now she doesn't? We're growing old out here! Which is it?"

Troy tucked his hands under his armpits and lowered his chin. "The dead lady's sister works part time for my mom. She's known her for a couple of years."

Anne felt a rush of relief. She might get to the bottom of this yet, hopefully without Gena yelling again. "Do you know her sister's name?"

"Elise."

"Elise what?" Anne asked.

Troy shrugged again, his shoulders nearly touching his ears. "I dunno."

"Do you know where she lives?"

Troy rubbed his nose. "How would I know that?"

Anne's leg suddenly felt stiffer than concrete. And just as heavy. "Well, maybe we'll come back when your mom's here."

When the three girls turned to go, Troy said in a cracked voice, "A-Anne? Can I talk to you for a minute?"

They all three stopped. When Anne realized he meant alone, she regretted coming over at all. Maybe she should have called. They stepped inside his living room while Juniper and Gena waited on the porch, no doubt trying to overhear what he had to say.

Troy looked down, fidgeting nervously. "I was thinking . . . I was thinking . . . thinking that . . . maybe when your leg gets better you and I could go to a movie together or something. You know . . . something." He rushed the last part and spoke so quietly she could barely hear him. He still stared at the floor.

Anne's stomach did a splat like ice cream on pavement. She didn't want to go anywhere with Troy, but she didn't want to hurt his feelings either. For once, her mom's old-fashioned views came in handy. "That would be fun," she said. "But my mom won't let me go out with boys yet. She thinks I'm too young."

He nodded, still staring at his feet.

"I'll see you at school," she said, heading out. The girls got on their bikes and rode to the corner, Gena grinning the whole time. At the stop sign, they formed a tight circle.

"Did he propose?" Gena asked.

Anne grinned back at her. "No, he just wanted to know if you'd go out with him. I told him you'd written his name all over your books. Then I gave him your phone number."

The look Gena gave her had yucky written all over it. "Oh, too bad. I plan to be in a coma when he calls."

Juniper leaned forward on her handlebars. "What are we doing?"

Anne drooped across hers. "I don't know. But for some reason, I need to find out who Alice Lang was."

"But why?" Juniper asked. "Why is it so important to you?"

Anne couldn't answer. She wished she knew. Gena took off her bike helmet and tugged her ponytail, tightening the band. "Let's go back to Anne's and consult the Hand of Fate. After all, we are the Fortune Tellers Club, not private detectives. We've usually been able to find out what we need to know by reading cards or something."

Anne nodded. When Gena was serious, she made sense. Of course that was rare, and a little scary, but true. "Let's go," Anne said.

Gena readjusted her helmet on her head and they took off.

They turned onto Anne's street, still going slowly so she could keep up. As they inched their way up to the driveway, there stood Anne's mom, her arms crossed, her face sour.

“Uh, maybe now’s not a good time,” Juniper said. “How about we come back tonight?

“I don’t know,” Gena kidded. “From the look on Mrs. Donovan’s face, I think ten years from tonight would be more like it.”

“Later,” Juniper whispered.

As they rode off, so did Anne’s confidence. What was she going to tell Mom? She walked her bike up the lawn and toward the porch, limping toward Mom’s threatening frown.

CHAPTER 6

The Why Factor

"I hope you didn't break a stitch," Mom said, her mouth tight with concern.

"I didn't." Anne tried to walk past her to the front door, but Mom gently grasped her arm.

"Anne, let's go in and talk."

Anne didn't feel like talking. She only wanted to lie down. Mom followed her into the bedroom. Newspapers were still strewn around. Anne stacked them nicely and set them on the floor, then eased up onto her bed.

"I know you're upset about this weekend, and I don't blame you. But riding your bike the day after a surgery is just absurd. What possessed you to do something like that?"

Anne let out a cargo of pent-up breath. Her leg throbbed. Mom had certainly used the right word. What did possess her? She closed her eyes and saw the truck rolling toward her again. Would that image ever go away?

"Well?"

Anne opened her eyes. "I just wanted to get out." That was the best excuse she could come up with for now. She didn't want to answer questions. Her mind was full of too many questions of her own.

Mom placed a hand on Anne's forehead to check for a fever. "You're not yourself today. Maybe you should take a nap."

Anne sighed again. "I'm not sleepy."

"Do you want to watch TV?"

"No." She'd never felt this droopy in her life. She wondered if it was like jet lag, only in this case, it would be trauma lag.

Mom leaned forward and ran her fingers through Anne's sun-streaked hair. Without a word, she got up to go.

"Mom . . . wait."

Mom sat back on the bed. Her look reminded Anne of all the times she'd been sick and stayed home from school. Mom had always looked over her like this. Same thin smile, sparkling gray eyes, and soft expression. Anne took her hand and crisscrossed her fingers in Mom's clasp. "Why do people die?"

Mom chuckled. "That's a silly question!"

"Let me reword it then. Why do people die at certain times? How come everyone doesn't live to be old and gray?"

"Life is ironic. Death is just a part of life. You come, you go."

"But why is death the most important part of life?"

Mom gave her an odd look. "I don't think it is. Living is the most important part."

Anne sat up, quickly collecting her thoughts. "In that case, how come the police don't stop traffic for weddings and graduations? If that lady yesterday was getting married, I would be at cheer camp right now."

"Well, not too many people form a train of cars to go to weddings and graduations. That's just silly. And believe me, I'm sure everyone wishes that lady had been getting married instead."

Anne was feeling anxious again. She rubbed her face, trying to figure out how she could get the answers she needed. Mom had said *possessed.* That's exactly how she felt. Possessed, pushed, driven . . . but who was doing the driving? And why were they steering her in this direction?

"Just get some rest and stop thinking about the accident," Mom said, patting Anne's arm. "No one said life was fair."

Anne laid her arm across her eyes. "It certainly isn't!"

She heard Mom quietly close the bedroom door. Reaching over, she picked up the Hand of Fate, squishing and kneading it like clay. Gena was right. *We're the Fortune Tellers Club. We've always been able to solve problems with divination.* Laying the hand flat, she flipped the coin.

It landed on the index finger. Juniper had written in blue marker *Fate will point the way.*

"I hope so," Anne said to herself. She picked up her kitty-cat phone and called Juniper's house. The answering machine clicked on. Anne didn't leave a message. She dialed Gena's.

"Hello," Gena said, her voice sounding anxious.

"What are you doing?" Anne asked.

"What are *we* doing? What about *you?* Are you in trouble? Are you grounded? Did your mom hang you up by your thumbs?" Gena rattled the questions off at warp speed.

Anne laughed. "I'm not grounded. I've never been grounded."

"You've never hidden math grades from your dad either," Gena said with authority.

Anne rolled over, a small cramp overtaking her calf. "We need to have a real meeting," she said. "Can you and Juniper come back over?"

Anne heard Gena's muffled voice as she conferred with Juniper. "Uh, we're not going to get a lecture from your mom about the hazards of riding a bike after an operation, are we?"

"No, but you'll get one from me if you don't get back over here."

"Yes, ma'am!" Gena shouted in a pitiful military voice. She didn't even say bye before hanging up.

* * *

It wasn't long until she heard them ringing the doorbell, but it seemed an eternity before they slipped quietly into her room, neither saying anything.

"What did my mom say?" Anne asked, when she saw them looking guilty.

"What didn't she say?" Gena said. "I thought you said there'd be no lecture!"

Juniper leaned against the bedpost and swatted at the ruffle hanging from the canopy. "She said we shouldn't have been out riding. She said you needed rest. Oh, and if you want to go out again, we are not to encourage you."

"I tried to tell her it was all your idea. That you made us do it," Gena said. "But she still thinks we're a bad influence." She grinned.

"She doesn't think that," Anne said, trying to prop herself up in the bed. "If she did, you wouldn't be in here right now."

"Why are we here?" Juniper asked. "You called a meeting. You must have some new idea about this lady who died."

Anne did. "I've been thinking about fate. What if I'd gone to camp?"

Gena held her nose. "You'd have had to smell Beth's cheesy perfume."

"No, really! Would something worse have happened to me if I'd gone? Did this lady die to protect me from something?"

Gena shrugged. "The cheerleaders could have missed catching you during a basket toss, and you could have hit the floor and broken your neck. Or worse, you could have suffocated smelling Beth's perfume."

"That's my point!" Anne said. "I think she died to save me."

"But she didn't even know you," Juniper added. "Why would she do that?"

Anne felt the desperation rise in her again. She couldn't hold it back. "That's what I need to find out."

Juniper sat down next to Anne, her face expressing confusion. "It seems to me that Alice Lang would choose to die at a time when she could help someone she actually knew. Someone she really cared about. I mean, get realistic, dying to save someone is a sacrifice. That would take true love."

"Fate's a funny thing!" Gena said, pointing a finger in the air.

"Maybe she did care about me," Anne said. "I think somehow, on some invisible cosmic realm, she and I are connected."

CHAPTER 7

The Séance

"Connected?" Juniper said, her eyes searching for a meaning.

"I can't explain it," Anne said. "It's just something I feel. Wait . . . I don't just feel it, I know it."

Anne wished she had a better way to explain it . . . to reveal how she truly felt. Her link to Alice Lang seemed as real as her membership in the Fortune Tellers Club.

Juniper tucked her hair behind her ears. "Connected? Like soul mates?"

"Or in this case, fate mates," Gena said.

Anne rolled her eyes and nodded. "Yeah, something like that."

"Well, why are we just sitting here?" Juniper asked. "Don't you think we should find some answers?"

Now we're getting somewhere, Anne thought, sitting up straight. "Yes, I need answers."

"How?" Gena asked.

Juniper looked at Anne. Anne picked up the Hand of Fate and squished the palm. "Guess we could use this?"

Juniper shook her head. "Let's think for a minute. Someone died. Her death has made a huge impact on you. She totally screwed up your weekend, and you think she did it for a reason."

"Right," Anne said, not sure where Juniper was going with this.

"So wouldn't it make sense to ask the dead woman herself?" Juniper asked.

Gena leaned in, her expression unsure. "The Ouija board?"

"No," Juniper said. "A séance!"

"No! Yes!" Gena and Anne's shouts rang out at the same time.

"We are not inviting Miss Cheer Wrecker here from beyond the grave!" Gena's eyes flamed with panic. "What if she decides to do more damage?"

Anne squeezed the Hand of Fate tight. A séance was the perfect solution. "I need answers, Gena. Juniper's right. If we can bring her here, maybe we can find out what's going on."

"What if we find out something we don't want to know? What if she doesn't leave? What if she follows me home?"

"Oh, grow up," Juniper said. "If she's connected to Anne, why would she follow *you* home?"

Gena picked up the teddy bear on Anne's bed and held it to her chest. "I wouldn't want to risk it."

"Why not?" Anne said, limping to the dresser. "Maybe she'll clean your room."

Juniper laughed. "Yeah, and when she's done with that, she can do your homework."

"Ha! Not a ghost of a chance," Gena said.

Anne came back, holding a pink heart-shaped candle on a small crystal dish. It had been a valentine gift from one of the boys at school, but Anne couldn't remember who. She got more than her share of valentines.

"Pink?" Gena asked. "We're going to conduct a séance with a pink candle? Not that I'm thrilled about this, and I'm still considering making a run for it, but pink?"

"It's the only candle I own." Anne closed the lace curtains on the windows, wishing they were thicker. The afternoon sun was still too bright.

Juniper turned out the bedroom light.

They sat in a circle on the floor, Anne trying to find a comfortable position for her hurt leg. Juniper struck a match.

The room seemed dark enough. The flame sent shadows dancing on the walls. Her dolls' shiny faces eclipsed like moons. And their silhouettes grew to an enormous size.

Anne stared into the still fire. "I think we should hold hands."

No one spoke. Gena and Juniper reached out. Anne clasped their hands.

Silence filled the room like a brisk chill. Anne wasn't sure what to do. This was her first séance. And as far as she knew, it was the Fortune Tellers Club's first séance too. Juniper had never mentioned participating in one. And Gena . . . well . . . that was obvious. "Should one of us speak to her?" Anne whispered.

Although all three girls had their heads down, their eyes were shifting back and forth, looking from one to the other. Anne felt Gena's grip grow tighter.

"Maybe you should call on her," Juniper finally whispered back. "I'm getting that strange vibe I get when something psychic is about to happen."

Gena rattled her head in a nervous nod.

Anne drew in a deep breath. She slowly let it out, relaxing her muscles as she did. She let her eyes drift closed, and took another deep breath. The truck tumbled toward her for a moment, but she quickly shut the image out. It was the hearse that she saw in her mind now. And the Hand of Fate. *Odd.*

Anne spoke softly. "We're trying to contact the spirit of Alice Lang. Alice Lang, can you hear me? Alice, we need to reach you. Please."

More silence, except for the sound of Gena's ragged breaths. Anne tried to loosen Gena's grip as a signal to relax. Gena clasped it even tighter.

"Alice," Anne continued, "please come forward. We're calling on Alice Lang. Please make your presence known."

The sound of the candle caused Anne to open her eyes. The flame sparked, dimmed, and sparked again.

"Did you see that?" Gena whispered, crushing Anne's hand.

Boy, if Gena was this scared now, she'd have been hysterical if we'd waited until dark, thought Anne.

The flame dipped.

"Aw!" Gena gasped.

"Shhhh!" Juniper's shushing carried an annoyed tone.

Good, Anne thought. She closed her eyes again. "Alice, are you here?"

Nothing. No sound. No crackles from the candle. Juniper spoke now. "Alice Lang, give us a sign. Let us know if you're here."

Still nothing . . . except . . .

"Do you smell that?" Juniper asked in an anxious whisper.

"It wasn't me," Gena said with a nervous giggle. "Be serious!" Juniper snapped in a tight murmur. "Don't you smell it?"

Anne could smell it. A familiar smell, but one she didn't smell often. "What is that?"

All three sat still, sniffing the air. Then it occurred to Anne. "It's baby powder. It smells just like baby powder."

"Yes," Juniper agreed.

Anne soaked the smell in. It was glorious. Relaxing, she closed her eyes again. "Alice, is that you?"

She wasn't sure what kind of answer she expected to get. How do the dead communicate? Baby powder? Would that be it? It certainly beat sniffing the smell of death, which Anne imagined would be sour and stale and dank, like wet sneakers left in a gym locker over the weekend.

"Alice, if this is you, I have to know about you. I think we're connected, somehow. Can you give me a clue?'

She was beginning to think Gena's Ouija board idea would have been better. At least Alice could have spelled out the answers.

"Alice," Juniper whispered, her voice shaky. "If you're here, make the flame rise on the candle."

The Fortune Tellers Club simultaneously lowered their heads and eyes toward the candle. Anne waited. Within a few seconds, the flames rose a little.

"She's here," Anne said. She gasped for breath, not so much from fear, but from the presence itself. Anne felt it wrap around her like a fuzzy blanket. *Is this what happens after death? We become a warm, fuzzy ball roaming an invisible world?* She calmed at the thought.

Now Juniper's grip was as tight as Gena's. Anne tried to relax her fingers—to send the cozy vibes she felt into Juniper and Gena too. *No one should be afraid. Not of this spirit.* But her efforts seemed hopeless as both girls continued to squeeze and tremble.

Juniper let out a shaky sigh. "Alice, we'd like to ask you some questions. Raise the flame for yes, and dim it for no."

Anne thought that was a perfect solution. "Alice," she said. "Are we connected?"

The flame grew a little taller. It stood tall and thin like a yellow-orange straw. The question seemed silly since Anne already knew the answer, but it was a double relief having it confirmed.

"Did I know you?"

The flame dimmed, then grew, then dimmed. Anne puzzled over it. *What does that mean?*

"Did you know me?"

The flame stood tall again.

Anne was aware that no one was breathing. She let out a soft breath, afraid that exhaling might affect the flame. "How did you know me?"

Anne knew Alice couldn't answer that question with the flame. She had to reword it. "Can you show me how you knew me? Can you give me an answer? I really need to know why you died. Why I'm not Cheerleader of the Year. Why this whole connection thing is eating at my brain."

The flame sputtered and sparked–rising, falling, nearly going out. Then a loud shrill "meow" pierced the silence, causing all three girls to jump in surprise. The kitty-cat phone rang again. Anne pulled her hands free and clutched her chest. The candle flame died, leaving a tiny trail of gray smoke.

Anne heaved as she grabbed the phone on the third ring. "Hello?"

"Is this Anne?" a boy said from the other end.

"Yes."

"This is Troy."

Anne could still feel her heart raging, just like when the truck rolled at her. "Yes," she said, trying to catch her breath.

"Remember you asked me about that lady that died. And I told you her sister worked for my mom?"

"Of course," Anne said. She could see Juniper motioning a "Who is it?", but Anne ignored her.

"Well," Troy went on. "My mom came home just now."

"And?" Anne asked.

"And I asked her about that stuff you asked me."

"What did she say?"

Troy hesitated. "She wanted to know why you wanted to know."

Anne scratched her head, trying to think and stay calm at the same time. "Oh . . . I just want to pay my respects to her sister." That seemed like a good innocent lie.

"Okay," Troy said.

Anne could practically hear him fidgeting on the other end. "Anyway, she said that her name is Elise Thurston, and she lives at 226 Circle Center."

"Wait!" Anne said, practically hurling herself to her night table to grab a pen. She wrote the name and address on the top portion of an obituary. "Thanks! I owe you."

"Great!"

Anne didn't care for his enthusiasm about that last reply, but she'd worry about it later.

Gena, who appeared much calmer now, said, "I take it that wasn't Alice calling from the great beyond to give you all those answers."

Anne thought about that. Maybe, in a way, it was.

CHAPTER 8

Fate's Door

"Okay," Gena said. "Let's look at this realistically."

Juniper looked surprised. "Since when are *you* realistic?"

Gena cleared her throat. "Bear with me." She took on the tone of a teacher just about to give an important test review. "Now let's suppose that by some miracle your mother lets you out of the house. And let's suppose that you do find where this Elise Thurston lives. Now, suppose if you will, that Elise is the type to invite a strange girl in to discuss the life and death of her beloved sister. Are you with me so far? Now suppose you have all this information that has set you on edge since the car wreck yesterday. Do you really think that you'll find the answers that you truly seek?"

Anne slumped and rolled her eyes. "What are you really asking, Gena?"

"How is that Elise lady going to know what psychic connection you had with her sister? She's going to think you're nuts!"

Juniper cleared her throat. "Not necessarily. Suppose Anne does find all the answers she needs. Suppose she's satisfied with them. Suppose we can then get on with our lives."

Anne wasn't sure what to make of Juniper's comments. "Hey! Whose side are you on?"

"Yours," Juniper said. "I know what it's like to have a psychic link. I've been there. I know how it eats at you. We'll all be better off once you find out what you need to know."

Anne relaxed. Juniper had a point. The trick was how to find Elise Thurston.

She opened the bedroom curtains, but no extra light filtered in. "It's too late to do any thing now. We'll have to wait until tomorrow."

Gena grinned. "We? I guess tomorrow we'll be paying a visit to Elise Thurston."

"You don't have to go," Juniper offered. "Anne and I can take care of it."

"Are you kidding?" Gena said. "After that freaky séance and the dancing candlelight, I'm not missing a thing."

Anne settled back on the bed with a smile. "Yeah. Our first séance. I'd say it was successful."

"You know what would really top it off?" Juniper asked with a sly grin. "If the ghost really does follow Gena home."

"Oh, thanks a lot!" Gena said, her face white as milk. "And I was just getting over my chilly-willies."

Anne picked up the Hand of Fate. "Don't worry. She's not going anywhere. Remember . . . she's connected to me."

When Anne woke the next morning, her leg didn't hurt as bad, but it still felt stiff. Her biggest goal was to walk normally and convince her parents she was fine. She practiced stepping across the room. It wasn't easy. She felt like she was dragging her left leg through a river of glue. She figured it was like gymnastics. You had to warm up. After a while her leg did relax enough to make her gait seem more natural.

"Well, look at you!" her dad said, lowering his Sunday paper. "If it wasn't for that bandage on your leg, I'd say you were as good as new."

And if it wasn't for that funeral, I'd be Cheerleader of the Year. She smiled at him. "And I feel great." *What a fib!*

"Oh, honey, that's so nice to hear."

Anne took a blueberry muffin from the tin and bit into it. It was still warm, giving it the familiar Sunday-morning flavor that she loved. "Where's Mom?"

"She had some dealings at church this morning. I think mostly she wanted to say thanks to the powers that be. She's carried on and on since Friday night about how lucky we are that things didn't turn out worse," her dad said.

Anne nodded. Her heart felt as warm as the muffin. She was glad things hadn't turned out worse too. Not just for her sake, but also for her parents. She couldn't bear to think of them in any emotional pain. Of course, that just made it harder for her to do what she had to do.

"Dad, isn't Circle Center close by?"

"Circle Center?"

"You know, the street."

Dad turned the page on the paper, not looking her way. "Circle Center is that cul-de-sac in the old neighborhood. I grew up near there."

"You mean that rundown area by the old lumberyard?"

"No," Dad said, shaking his head. He stopped to sip some coffee. "It's over where the old high school used to be. Isn't that a daycare center now?" His last question didn't seem to be directed to her.

Anne perked up. She knew just where he meant, and though it would be a painful bike ride, she could take a rest break at Juniper's house first. Her place was a bit closer to the old high school. "Since I'm feeling better, I think I'll ride over to Juniper's . . . okay?"

Dad was transfixed on some sports article. "Uh-hum."

"Great! Love you, Dad!"

Anne waited until he left the kitchen before limping back to her room. She called Juniper on the phone. "It's all set. I'll be leaving as soon as I'm dressed."

"You know where Elise Thurston lives?" Juniper asked.

"About. We can find it. Anyway, I have to hurry before my mom gets home from church."

The ride to Juniper's was less painful than she expected. She didn't really want to rest there after all, except they did have to wait on Gena. She finally rode up.

"Let's roll!" Anne said.

The Sunday morning traffic was heavy, but no one appeared to be in a hurry. When they crossed a busy intersection, Anne found her leg stiffening again as images of the rolling truck snapped in her thoughts. She shook them off and kept going. She also couldn't help but wonder what her mom would think if she knew what she was up to right now. It would probably result in being grounded for the first time. They walked their bikes across the street, just under the red light, and then rode on.

"Are you sure you know where we're going?" Gena asked, huffing from the long ride.

"No," Anne said with a giggle. "Just help me figure out exactly where the old high school is."

Juniper pointed to the right. "It's that way."

They pushed off and headed that direction.

The streets started looking alike—narrow lanes, cars parked on the road, small brick homes with faded paint and dull gray shingles. Anne remembered Dad driving her through here once, showing her the house he grew up in "umpteen years ago," as he put it. She wasn't sure how many "umpteen" was, but it was one of his favorite words.

They were cycling through a maze. Up and down, street after street. No cul-de-sacs. Finally they came upon a small park, and just beyond, the old high school.

"We're in the right area," Juniper said. "If we zigzag enough, we should find it."

Gena sighed. "Hopefully in this century."

Anne didn't say anything. She just led the way. A few minutes later, they turned onto a street called Circle Drive. About halfway down was the cul-de-sac.

It was a tiny circle of a road, lined with bushes and full of cars. Anne spotted 226—a quaint yellow house with white trim. It looked cheery against the dark morning rain clouds that had gathered suddenly. And Anne figured the house had to be at least umpteen years old.

They walked their bikes up the sidewalk. Anne didn't hesitate. She'd come this far. She'd made it. There was no backing out.

Juniper and Gena stood by as Anne pressed the doorbell. It buzzed rather than rang. *Please be home!* she thought.

The door opened to reveal a petite, young woman with dark blonde hair, and a soft expression—an expression that turned to shock when she saw Anne. She stared through large teary blue eyes. "Oh no. You're here."

CHAPTER 9

Alice's Wonderland

"Yes," Anne said, not sure why the woman would say that.

The lady closed her eyes and shook her head, as though erasing the words Anne had spoken. She opened her eyes and took a deep breath. "I'm sorry. I—uh—can I help you?"

Juniper and Gena turned toward Anne. The silence hung thick for a moment, then Anne said, "Are you Elise Thurston?"

"Yes," the woman said, her face tight as a rock.

"My name is Anne, and I was involved in the accident on Friday." She turned and showed the bandage on her leg.

The woman closed her eyes again. Her hands were tight fists. "Oh dear." She swooned a little, then opened her eyes. "This has been a horrible weekend for me."

"I'm sorry, Miss Thurston," Anne said. "I just had some questions about your sister."

Elise Thurston popped her head up, chin firm. She took another breath, then ran her fingers through her golden hair. "Maybe you should come in."

Gena clutched Anne's arm, holding her back. "It's okay," Anne whispered. "She works for Mrs. Messina. How dangerous can she be?"

The girls followed Elise Thurston into the house. The front room was much bigger than Anne had expected when compared to the outside of the house. There were hardwood floors and scattered throw rugs, lots of tables with magazines, and decorative candles sitting about. This was definitely a woman's house.

"Miss Thurston," Anne started, sitting on the dark gold couch.

"Call me Elise, please. Miss Thurston makes me sound old, or like I'm a school teacher or something." For the first time, she smiled.

"Okay . . . Elise . . ." Anne's thoughts stammered. Now that she was here, she wasn't sure how to ask all the questions that had been smothering her for the last couple of days.

Juniper, standing behind the couch, spoke up. "Why did you say, 'You're here' when you first saw Anne?"

Anne didn't like Juniper butting in, but she did ask a great question.

Elise blushed a rosy shade of pink. "Oh, forget that. I thought you were someone else."

"Anyway," Anne said, "This is Juniper and Gena. We're here to get some information."

"Yes. You wanted to know about my sister. What did you want to know?"

"I want to know why she died," Anne asked quickly.

"Alice had a rare form of cancer. She lived with it for about twelve years or so. She was lucky to have lived that long. And I was lucky she did. It's going to be so lonesome here without her." Tears swelled in the lower parts of her eyes, but they never spilled over.

"She was kind of young, wasn't she?" Anne asked.

"Yes. And lively for a dying woman. See that painting by the window? She did that. She could see colors like no other person in the world." Elise looked at the painting like she were living inside it.

Anne had to admit, the painting was fantastic. A very realistic spider web was draped from a blooming dogwood tree. Surrounding the tree were clumps of radiant flowers. But the uniqueness of this picture was the tiny blonde woman in a honey-colored gown, sleeping on the spider's web.

Gena stepped up to the painting and leaned toward it, examining every detail. Anne wished she would sit down. Gena had been pacing like a cat ever since they'd walked in, touching every knick-knack on every shelf and table. Anne wanted to scream, "Give it a rest, Sherlock!" But instead, she focused her attention back on Elise.

"She must have been very special."

Elise nodded. This time a tear trickled. "There is a certain beauty in suffering. Alice lost so much in her short time here. So much." These words were not directed at anyone.

"Your last name is Thurston, but Alice's was Lang. Was she married?"

"For a short time. She married Bob Lang, her high-school sweetheart. They got married just after graduation. About a year later she found out she was sick. The treatments were horrible. Bob couldn't take it. Big star running back of the high-school football team couldn't handle the pressure of dealing with a terminally ill wife. He left."

"That's awful!" Anne blurted. "What a pig."

Elise grinned. "That's one of the nicer names he's been called. Anyway, he rode off into the sunset. We've never heard from him since the divorce papers were signed."

Anne suddenly felt like a trespasser. So many personal questions. Still, she was eager to know more. "Was Alice a–uh–what's the word . . . a sensitive person?" She knew that wasn't exactly the word she wanted to use, but she figured caution was best.

"If you mean did she love animals and children and taking pleasure in other's achievements, then yes, there was no one more sensitive."

Juniper leaned forward, resting her arms on the back of the couch. "I think Anne wants to know if Alice was psychic."

So much for caution! Anne cringed at Juniper's blunt question. But Elise nodded slightly, considering the question.

"Not really psychic, but she knew things. Odd things."

“Do you mind if we ask what kind of odd things?” Anne asked, burning to know, yet trying to stay calm and polite.

“She could predict the weather without hearing any forecasts. I trusted her more than the TV weatherman.”

“That’s kinda cool,” Juniper chimed.

“I hated watching mystery movies with her though. She always solved them halfway through. And I mean really solved them, no guessing. Same thing with books.”

“So she liked to read?” Anne asked.

“She loved to read. Mostly the classics, and some poetry. I teased her about how boring they were. I tried to get her to read *The National Enquirer,* you know, just to spice things up, but she said she couldn’t waste any time on rubbish. The weird thing is, toward the end, she took to reading children’s books.” Elise raised her eye brows expressing how odd that seemed.

“Back to the psychic thing,” Juniper said, her words hurried. “Did she ever solve any real-life mysteries?”

Elise turned to look at Juniper. Her face looked drawn, her color pale. Without batting an eyelash she said, “She knew our parents had been killed moments before the phone rang to notify us.”

Even Gena stopped dallying at those words. Anne didn’t know quite what to say. So far she’d learned that Alice was a young woman who loved the arts, the classics, nature, and was sensitive to her surroundings. And yes, she was psychic. But this didn’t answer anything about their connection with each other. A clock chimed on the mantle, bringing her back to reality.

Anne scooted closer to Elise. “That must have been really hard on you. How old were you when they died?”

Elise closed her eyes and scratched her forehead. “I was eight. Alice was fifteen.”

She rubbed her face as if all the questions had suddenly overwhelmed her. “I’m sorry. I’m not a very good host. Can I get you something to drink? A soda or some red punch?”

Anne was about to decline when Gena blurted, "I'd love some red punch."

"Anyone else?" Said

Elise got up and hurried into the kitchen. Gena rushed over to the couch. In her softest voice she whispered, "This is creepy, Anne. Let's drink the punch and go!"

"Oh, you're scared of everything, Gena," Anne whispered back. "Quit being such a drama queen."

"Me? Look who's sitting in a stranger's house, asking questions about a dead girl she's never met, but is sure she's linked to on some outer realm. Even Shakespeare couldn't write this drama."

"I think we've learned as much as we can today," Juniper murmured a little louder than the others. "I'm with Gena. Let's give this lady a rest."

Elise walked back in with three paper cups of punch. "Here you go."

Anne stood up to retrieve hers. They sipped and looked about. Gena went back to her dawdling about the room. Juniper joined her.

"Thank you for answering my questions," Anne said. "It's probably not easy for you right now."

Elise smiled at Anne, her eyelids narrowed. "I don't mind. I think you should know how special Alice was. She would have liked that you came by."

Anne felt the shiver of an invisible chill. She downed her punch, and handed Elise the empty cup.

Gathering Juniper and Gena's cups, Elise said, "I'll be right back."

Gena motioned toward Anne. "Pssssst! Quick! Come here!"

What now? Anne walked to where Gena and Juniper stood. Juniper's gaze was fixed on the mantle, staring hard.

Gena backed away, nodding toward the picture Juniper stared at. "I think we found the connection."

There in the picture stood two girls. One about five, dressed in a one-piece pink romper with tiny elephant buttons. Another girl, about twelve or so, stood next to her. Long blond hair. Clear blue eyes. Anne nearly fainted when she saw her. She gripped the mantle for support. *It's impossible.* This girl could have been her clone!

CHAPTER 10

It's in the Stars

"So why didn't you ask her about the picture?" Gena said as they stopped on the next street corner to talk.

Anne still felt jittery and cold from the whole thing. "I was afraid to. Besides, I got my answer, didn't I? Did you see her? That had to be Alice. Did you see her?" She tried to keep the panic out of her voice, but it spilled over like bubbling soda.

"Did we *see* her?" Gena said. "Anne, I'm looking at her now. That girl was your twin."

Juniper reached out, still balancing her bike with her knees. She clasped Anne's arm. "We've got to find out how this is possible. She has to be your cousin or something. Maybe on your mom's side."

Anne shook her head. "I know all my cousins on both sides. They're all grown-ups. None of them look like me."

Gena sat back on her bike seat, one foot on the pedal, the other resting on the ground. "You don't have any cousins your age?"

Anne shook her head. How could Alice be her cousin? That's impossible.

"No cousins your age?" Gena went on. "You're so lucky! No bratty boy cousins to trip you or wrestle you down? No prissy girl cousins who think they're beauty queens? Where do I sign up for *that* family reunion?"

Anne shrugged. She looked at Juniper. "This is crazy. There's got to be a good explanation for all this."

"There is," Juniper said. "Haven't you heard that everyone has a twin somewhere in the world?"

"But what are the odds that my twin would be in the same town as me?" Anne asked. "And what are the odds that I'd find out this way?"

Juniper clasped the handlebars on her bike. "Fate?"

Anne didn't think she ever wanted to hear that word again.

"Come on," Juniper said. "Let's go back to my house. I have an idea."

* * *

The ride back didn't seem nearly as long. Anne's leg was starting to ache and sting at the same time, and a funny taste settled in her mouth. A salty taste. She took that as a warning to rest. When they reached Juniper's house, she was limping again—much more than before.

"So what's the idea?" Anne asked, sipping a cool glass of water.

Gena quickly piped in. "Nothing creepy, okay? I'm already having nightmares from that major conjuring session we had yesterday. Last night I dreamed Alice came and took me to Wonderland.

Only it turned out to be a spook house, complete with zombie teachers and autopsy exams."

Juniper giggled. "That nightmare wasn't because of the séance. That was a school dream. Maybe if you studied more, you could *rest in peace.*"

Anne and Juniper both laughed out loud.

Gena smirked. "Not funny!"

"Anyway," Juniper said. "I think the answer lies in the stars."

"Astrology?" Anne asked.

Juniper nodded.

Gena perked up at this. "That sounds cool. We've never done our charts or anything."

"I have some astrology books," Anne said, but I only know my sun sign. I'm a Libra. Should we go get my books?"

Juniper stood up. "There's a better way." She crossed the room to her desk computer, and scrambled the mouse around for a minute. "We can get a free chart done on the internet."

"Awesome!" Gena blurted. "Can we do mine too?"

"I'm first," Anne said. "We have to solve this." They waited. Anne heard the beeping and the buzzing as the modem connected.

"Here we go," Juniper said at last.

They gathered around the monitor, watching the graphics of stars and planets shoot across the screen. Then a questionnaire popped up. Juniper read each question out loud as she typed. "Name. Date of birth. Place of birth. Time of birth." That's where she stopped. "What time were you born?"

"I have no idea," Anne said. "Why do they need to know that?"

Juniper slumped. "It has to be precise. And in this case, very precise."

"I'll call my mom and ask her."

"I'll have to disconnect," Juniper said. "We only have one phone line."

Gena brought the phone over to Anne so she wouldn't have to get up. Her leg not only throbbed—she could see some swelling around the bandage.

"Hello?" her father said.

"Dad? Is Mom home yet?"

"Nope, not yet. Are you still at Juniper's?"

"Yes, and I need to know something. What time of day was I born?"

This left a crater of silence on the other end. Anne waited. "Dad? Do you know?"

"I'm trying to remember," he said. "I don't think anyone ever told me."

"When do you think Mom will be home? She ought to know."

"Not for a while. She called and said for us to have sandwiches for lunch and she'd be home in time to cook dinner. You know her. She gets around those church women, and they find all kinds of things to get into."

Anne's spirit sank like a rock. "Thanks, Dad. I'll be home later." She hung up the phone and set it down on the desk. "No good. He doesn't know and Mom's not home."

"What if your Mom doesn't know?" Gena said. "You may not be able to get your chart done at all."

Anne tossed Gena a look. "She has to know, silly. She was there!"

"So do we wait till tomorrow then?" Juniper said, rolling the mouse around in circles.

"I don't want to wait," Anne whined. "Not tomorrow, not even tonight. I have to find out about Alice now before I go completely batty!"

"Calm down," Gena said. "I know another way."

"Really?"

Juniper turned to Gena. "This better be serious." Gena arched her eyebrows with pride. "Where there's a birth, there's a birth certificate."

"Will it have the time of birth?" Anne asked.

"Mine does," Gena said.

Juniper scooted back in her chair. "Gena has a good idea. You could go home real fast and check your birth certificate. Then call me, and I'll have your chart ready when you get back."

Anne smiled and rubbed her leg. "I don't think I can do anything *real fast* right now, but this is perfect."

"You want me to come with you?" Gena asked.

Anne considered it. "I think I'll be able to do it quicker alone. You can stay and double-check Juniper's typing."

"Gena double-check me?" Juniper said. "Ha-ha. At least I know where the home keys are."

Gena playfully slapped her arm. "Well, smartie, maybe you should read all the questions on the internet before she gets back. Who knows, they may ask for her shot records too!"

"I'm only learning about my planets, not traveling to them!" Anne said with a giggle. And she hurried as quickly as her leg would let her, leaving Juniper's and pedaling home.

CHAPTER 11

Living a Lie

Anne's leg had taken more than it could handle within the last couple of hours. The pain was real, shooting in tiny spikes like someone lightly touching a match to her skin. She limped into the house.

"Want a sandwich?" Dad asked as she hurried through the living room.

"No thanks."

"I'm going to start calling you Hop-a-long!" he shouted toward the hallway.

"What?" Anne didn't have a clue as to what he meant, although she was sure it had something to do with her not being able to put pressure on her surgically mended leg. Her limp had turned into a hop after all. So much for the convincing act she'd put on earlier. There was just no walking normal now, even to fake out Dad.

She went straight into her parents' bedroom and opened the closet. The smell of her mother's talc enveloped her. It was the same smell that filled their bathroom as well. It was the only smell that drowned out Dad's Old Spice. Anne reached up to the closet shelf and clumsily fumbled for the small metal file box in the corner. She knew that was where all the important papers were kept. Her birth certificate had to be in there. Luckily, she was tall. Only last year she would have needed a stool to reach it. She inched it forward, and grabbed it before it could drop to the ground.

The box was heavier than she expected. She settled it on the carpet and carefully eased herself down in a sitting position. Indian style was out of the question now that her leg was screaming with pain. Lifting the lid, she found it crammed with all sorts of papers—military certificates, stock info, savings bonds. Several of the bonds had her name on them. She guessed they were part of her college fund that her parents always talked about. Or as Dad would say, "Securing the future."

She dug and flipped through a zillion things, wondering if maybe she should offer to clean out this box and organize it for her parents. Some of this stuff looked perfectly ancient and probably not worth anything anymore. Why in the world did they need to keep the receipt for a television/stereo combination they bought in 1977?

Anne thought this would be a breeze. Just pop it open and pull it out. She was getting more anxious by the moment. Then she found a brown envelope sealed tight with yellowed cellophane tape. The tape looked like it had been popped open a few times and resealed. It wasn't holding too well. Anne figured she'd hit the jackpot when she saw her dad's handwriting on the front. In small letters it said *Anne's papers.* She popped up the half-stuck tape and pulled out an official document. Hmmm . . . birth certificates were three pages long? She straightened it out, searching frantically for her time of birth. That's when she saw the label at the top of the document—Certificate of Adoption. Anne dropped the paper.

She paused. It had to be a mistake. Not hers at all. She picked it up again to examine it. This was a certificate for a nineteen-week-old baby named Haley Christine. Reading further she saw her parents names, Albert and Carolyn Donovan. Further down the page were the words that branded her. New name: Anne Elizabeth. Her!

She sat, numb, not even feeling the pain in her leg. Her breathing stopped. The world stopped. Her whole life stopped. Then slowly, a new sensation crept upon her, starting with her fingers . . . hands . . . arms . . . circulating through her like an electrical current. She began trembling and couldn't stop. Her stomach curled along with the jolting seizure. She couldn't stop shaking, but she wasn't sure if she wanted to. She wasn't sure about anything. Then just as slowly as the jitters had come on, she felt a scream welling in the pit of her nauseated stomach. It swelled higher and higher, like a balloon filling her insides and threatening to bust out her throat. She clamped her hands tightly over her mouth to hold it in. Her whole body was on vibrate as tears stung her eyes. Without thought of her injured leg, she pounded down the hall, and threw herself on her pillow, sobbing.

Who was she? Why was she here? The word *fate* popped into her head again, but she tossed it away like a child who'd outgrown a toy. She didn't hear the phone ring. There were no outside noises in the void of that moment. She clutched her pillow and soaked it with frenzied tears. Her father walked in.

"Gena's on the ph—" He tossed the telephone down on her wicker chair, and hurried to her in his own panic. "What's wrong, baby?"

Anne turned toward him, screaming, "YOU SHOULD HAVE TOLD ME! YOU SHOULD HAVE TOLD ME! YOU SHOULD HAVE TOLD!"

She lashed out, striking her father on the arms and chest. "You should have told me!" He swaddled her close, holding her tight against him. He rocked her as she continued to scream. "Told you what, baby? Told you what?"

She pulled herself loose, pushing her damp hair from her face. "I'm adopted!" The words echoed off the walls and pounded in her ears.

Her father's face lost color. His eyes dimmed. His look withered with guilt. He trembled too. "I'll call your mother. She should be here."

Mother? Who's mother? Those words seemed as strange as the ones on the vocabulary list she received every week in her English class. She wiped her eyes and cheeks, and ran her hand under her nose, wiping it too. She watched her Dad go back to the phone. *Dad?* Another odd word.

He started to dial, then listened. "Oh, Gena, I'm sorry. We'll have to call you back." He pressed the end button and dialed again.

Anne felt a headache drawing on. She rubbed her face again. Gena had heard. She'd heard it all. The screaming, the questions, the truth. It was no longer an ugly secret between her parents. *Parents?* She flung herself back on the pillow, fists clenched. She clamped her eyes shut, trying to black out the world that now turned backward for her. She was not Cheerleader of the Year. She was not Albert and Carolyn's miracle baby. She was not even Anne Elizabeth Donovan. She was not real. Her whole life was a lie.

CHAPTER 12

Fate Revealed

Anne was still lying on the bed when she heard her mother's car pull into the driveway. Her mind and spirit were hollow. She wasn't sure how to think and feel at the moment, other than drained.

Muffled voices spoke outside her door, then her mother and father entered, both approaching quietly and carefully, as though sneaking up on a wounded bird. Anne didn't react when her mom sat down next to her on the bed. She wanted an explanation, but she'd wait and let Mom speak first. Her dad took his place at the end of the bed, rubbing his wrinkled forehead with his hand.

"We're both so sorry, Anne." Her mother's voice quivered. "We had intended to tell you just after your thirteenth birthday. We thought thirteen would be the age you'd best be able to handle that information."

Anne spoke without movement. "My birthday was weeks ago. What were you waiting for?"

"The perfect time. If there is one. We wanted to ease you into it at a time when you didn't have a lot going on . . . like school or cheer squad or a holiday. I promise we would have told you. We would have."

Anne stayed still and listened. She didn't doubt any of what her mother said, but she wished they'd told her long, long ago. She didn't respond. Instead she just stared at the wall through tired, blurry eyes.

"Maybe she'd rather rest now," her dad said, getting up and trudging out of the room. Her mom stayed fixed on the spot next to Anne. She reached over and rubbed Anne's arm, then gave it a loving squeeze. She stood up and sighed.

As she turned to leave, Anne quietly asked, "Did you know my real mother?"

Mom sat back down. "No. I saw her once, but I was never introduced."

Anne turned toward her. "But somewhere out there, I have a real mother."

Another sigh. "Anne, there is more to being a mother than giving life to a child. Much more."

"So you're saying my real mother didn't want me?" She could see the hurt in her mom's eyes, but she didn't think it could compare to the hurt she felt. They had betrayed her.

"No. I wasn't saying that at all. Being a mother means doing the very best you can for your child. And if the best you can do is to turn her over to a family who can love her, and provide for her, and give her more of themselves than imaginable, then that's being a good mother."

Anne wondered if this was true. She'd like to think that her birth mother did what was right, instead of dumping her on someone else. Mom wiped a tear from her own cheek, sniffled, then rubbed Anne's arm again. "Albert and I thought life wasn't fair. We wanted a baby more than anything in the world. It was so hard watching all our friends and family with their children. Then we got you, and it was the greatest gift of our lives. You. You came to us, and it was like you were our own. And we couldn't love you more." Another tear trickled down her face.

"What happened to my *real* mother and father? Why did they give me away?"

"Your mother was young," Mom said. "And just before you were born she became ill. Terminally ill. She knew she couldn't take care of herself, her medical bills, and you. And she only had a short time to live. She couldn't give you a lifetime of care. She wanted to know you would be fine before she died."

Mom's words snapped in Anne's mind. Suddenly, this new gray world had color, and it all made sense. The funeral, the picture of her twin, and Elise Thurston saying, "You're here." Fate had stepped in again. Alice Lang was her real mother.

Mom must have seen the light in Anne's eyes. She brushed her hair aside and gazed at her with a puzzled look. "What are you thinking, sweetie?"

"I'm thinking about how life works. Life and death. What if that funeral hadn't taken place on Friday? I would be at cheer camp, and I'd still be Anne Donovan. But the funeral happened. And the wreck happened. And because of it I discovered who I really am."

"But you're still Anne Donovan. No matter what," Mom said. "You grew up here as Anne. You do gymnastics and cheerleading. You like all those silly fortune telling things." With those words she picked up the Hand of Fate and laid it down next to her. "You walk, talk, and think as Anne. There's no going back to who you were or could have been. You're Anne Elizabeth Donovan, Albert and Carolyn's baby girl. And as long as we're alive, that's always who you'll be."

Anne ran her fingers down the thick black lines drawn on the Hand of Fate—each one like an avenue. Juniper and Gena had made a small town where every street had Fate in its name. "Mom, could you or Dad drive me somewhere?"

Mom looked a bit worried. "I think you should rest. You've had a traumatic day."

"No, really," Anne said. "There's something I have to do. Someone I have to see."

"But tomorrow's a school holiday. Surely you can wait 'til then."

"No." Anne sat up. "I can't. I've waited too long already."

"May I ask who it is we'll be driving you to see?"

Anne gazed into her mother's eyes, giving her a loving look. "My aunt."

CHAPTER 13

Visiting the Past

Anne sat in the backseat of the car. Her dad drove while Mom stared straight ahead. No one spoke. The zoom of a passing car was the only thing that broke the uncomfortable silence.

Mom had insisted that Anne rest a while before leaving. But her head still felt groggy and her eyes were swollen from earlier tears. It all seemed like a dream. Anne would wake up on her cot at cheer camp, surrounded by squeaking sneakers and girly giggles. If only that were true.

When they reached the old high school, Anne told her dad which street to turn on. He slowly wound the steering wheel, creeping around the corner. This was no joy ride.

The little house yawned peacefully in the dusk of the setting sun. Anne looked at it for a minute, trying to collect her thoughts. Maybe Mom had been right. Maybe she should have waited until tomorrow. But tomorrow would bring a new light, and she wanted to settle things before she had time to change her mind.

"We'll wait here," Dad said, killing the engine. Anne stepped out and limped up to the front door. Taking a deep breath, she rang the buzzer.

The look on Elise Thurston's face held no surprise. She opened the door wide to let Anne in.

"I know," Anne said, barely above a whisper.

Elise smiled. "Me too."

Anne sat on the sofa, stretching out her injured leg. Elise sat across from her.

"You recognized me, huh?" Anne said.

"I recognized Alice." Elise nodded toward the picture on the mantle.

Anne looked down, fiddling with the hem of her shirt. "It's freaky. I look just like her."

Elise leaned forward, peering low to meet Anne's eyes. "Freaky is a great word for it. I do believe in reincarnation, but I knew there was no way Alice could come back as a teenage girl. There was only one other answer."

"Why didn't you say something while I was here earlier?"

Elise sighed. "What? What could I say?"

"You could have told me."

Elise leaned back. "At first I thought you knew. I thought that was the reason you came. But then, the more you talked, the more I realized you were just poking for answers about your injury. I loved answering your questions about Alice. She was so special."

Anne perked up at this. Special? Maybe to a sister, but not to a daughter. "Why was she special? Because she liked poetry and could solve mystery movies? Because you grew up with her? Because you shared things with her? In that case, wouldn't any sister be special?"

"Probably," Elise said, speaking softly. "But it was so much more. She was the most courageous woman I've ever known. I couldn't go through everything that she did and continue to live with a smile in my eyes. She never gave up."

"She gave up on me," Anne said quickly.

Elise flinched at those words. "No. She thought you were the world!"

"She gave me away."

"Anne, she was terrible sick. The doctors gave her just a few months to live. Who knew she'd fight to prove them wrong? She gave you away because she wanted you to be happy. You were the love of her life. Even after you were adopted, she would stare at your pictures and tell me how important you'd be one day. She spoke about you as though you were already grown, and elected as the first lady president or something. She said her whole reason for living was to have you. That you'd go on to make such a difference in the world. She was so convincing, I believed her."

Anne sat, a single tear threatening to fall. Now she felt a new burden. Living up to Alice's dreams. "I don't think I'll be solving all the world's problems, or bringing about world peace. I'm not an Einstein or anything."

"It doesn't matter," Elise said. "Alice would think you were special no matter what you do. She missed you so much when you left. It tore her heart out. We thought she'd die that day. It surprised us all when she lived twelve more years."

"Why didn't she try to find me?"

"She couldn't," Elise answered. "That's the rules of adoption."

"She had no idea where I was?"

Elise shook her head.

"What about my father? The no-good Bob Lang? Why didn't he want me?"

"It's complicated. He was young. He wasn't ready for any kind of commitment. Marriage, fatherhood, or taking care of a dying wife. He was never cruel, just immature."

They sat in silence. Anne thought about her parents out in the car, waiting. *Were they talking? What were they saying? How were they feeling?*

"Anne," Elise said, taking her hand. "I know this is hard for you. It's awkward for me too. I've rediscovered a niece I hadn't seen since she was a baby. It's painful for me."

"Wha–?" Anne's surprise was cut short.

"No! I don't mean meeting you has been painful. I know Alice would be so proud of you. It's painful for me to look at you. You're her. You're Alice. Every blond hair on your head. Every sparkle in your crystal blue eyes. Even the white moons on your fingernails. It's like going back in time for me. That's the painful part."

"I guess I should stay away." Anne didn't want to cause pain to anyone. Not Elise. Not her parents. Not Alice. Although she'd never understand why Alice had hurt her. Was it really necessary to crush her dreams of Cheerleader of the Year, just to clue her in on her true identity? Couldn't she have found an easier way?

Elise smiled slightly. "Stay away? That would be even more painful."

"It seems like either way I'll be hurting you," Anne said. "I can't help it if I look like her."

"I'm glad you do." Elise sat for a moment in thought. "What do your parents think? Will they be upset that you came here?"

Anne snickered under her breath. "They're outside."

Elise jumped up from the chair. "Let's invite them in!"

Anne hopped up too. "No. No. Uh—not yet." A slight pain seared the side of her leg. "I think I should go."

Elise nodded. "Yes. They've probably waited long enough."

"Not as long as me," Anne said, shrugging.

"Anne, would you like my phone number? Maybe you could call me sometime. We could go see a movie or have lunch together one weekend."

Anne liked the idea. "Okay."

Elise ripped a corner from the page of a magazine and scribbled a number on it. "Here. Give me a call when we're both over the shock."

Anne took the paper from her. "I will." And she knew that she would.

"If it's okay with your mother, the next time we get together we can go through Alice's stuff. I bet you'd like to have some of her things."

"I'd love it," Anne said. Her mind was still hazy, but the thought of owning just one piece of her real mother lit up her heart.

Just before she reached the door, Elise said, "Oh, wait." She went to the mantle and took down the picture that Anne had seen earlier. The one that had totally rattled her. "Take this." She handed the picture to Anne. "And remember," she said with a wink, "that silly-looking kid with the freckles is me."

CHAPTER 14

The Missing Puzzle Piece

Monday morning and no school! Kids would be out and about—the mall, the movies, eating ice cream at the Tasty Freeze. Anne dressed early even though she had no idea where to go. The impact of the weekend had taken a toll on her, but she wanted her life back. She needed to be in control again, and she felt she was on her way. The puzzle pieces had all been placed together and an easiness was settling in. Almost. Her injured leg was the constant reminder that there was still something missing. She sat in the living room, watching a talk show and snacking on cheese crackers. She had the Hand of Fate next to her, occasionally squeezing it like a cat toy. There was a light rapping at the front door. Anne didn't bother to get up, and her mom was there in a flash to answer it. She'd been hovering over Anne since yesterday.

Gena and Juniper crept in. They both walked slowly, carefully, looking at Anne like she was an endangered species. Anne wanted to spare them any awkward conversation. "So you heard me on the phone yesterday, huh?"

Gena nodded. "Are you really adopted?"

The word bristled the hairs on the back of her neck, but she shrugged off a chill. "I guess so."

Juniper sat on the couch next to her. "I'm sorry."

Anne thought that was odd. "It's not your fault."

"I mean about sending you home to look for your birth certificate. It's kind of my fault."

Anne snickered. "Actually, it's Gena's fault. It was her idea."

"Oh yeah," Gena said, "Blame it on me! I was only trying to help. I have one brilliant idea and–"

Anne threw a cheese cracker at Gena, hitting her arm. "Get a sense of humor. I'm just pulling your leg."

"Well, you sure don't want me pulling yours," Gena said, pointing to the wound on Anne's leg. "And why don't you have a bandage on that? It looks gross!"

"Then don't look at it," Anne answered.

"Okay, I won't!" Gena picked up the cheese cracker and shot it back at Anne. Anne ducked, but it still bounced off her shoulder and landed in her lap.

Juniper reached for the Hand of Fate. "Any questions?"

"Yeah," Gena said. "What are we going to do today?"

"I'm sitting right here," Anne said. "My mom's been watching every move I make. She's not about to let me back on my bike today."

Gena clapped her hands together then pointed to Anne. "Ah ha! You're grounded."

Anne scooched back and propped her leg on the coffee table. "Something like that."

Just then the doorbell rang. Just as quickly it rang again.

"I got it." Juniper jogged over and opened the front door. Beth Wilson pushed her way through, shoving Juniper aside.

"How are you feeling?" Beth plopped herself down next to Anne, in the spot where Juniper had just been sitting.

"I'm fine."

Anne barely got the words out before Beth started in. "Omigosh, Anne, you should have seen it! The whole place was in chaos."

"What?"

Again Beth interrupted. "The weekend was so much fun, then to have that happen. Can you believe it?"

"Believe what?" Anne sat up straight, her curiosity itching.

"You didn't hear?"

"Beth," Gena said, leaning forward. "Pretend for one brief moment that we don't live in your insane world. If you want an answer, you have to clue us in."

"I wasn't talking to you." Beth smirked a fake grin. "And besides, you'd still be clueless even if I wrote it out for you."

"Probably because I can't make out your handwriting. I'm still wondering in what grade they taught us to dot an *i* with a heart or smiling face."

Anne threw her hands in the air to signal a time-out. "Enough! Beth, what chaos are you talking about?"

Beth readjusted herself on the couch, sitting on her leg and leaning toward Anne. "The awards ceremony. You should have seen it."

"Who won Cheerleader of the Year?" Juniper asked.

Beth turned to Juniper and gave her the same smirky grin. "Will you just let me tell it?"

Juniper raised her hands in surrender.

"Susan won Cheerleader of the Year."

"That's no surprise," Anne said. "She is Cheer Captain."

"Wait. You haven't heard the worst part. While they were handing out the awards, they had everyone stand under the basketball backboard in the gym. We were all sitting on the floor, and a bunch of the parents were sitting on the bleachers. As Susan got up to get the Cheerleader of the Year trophy, the hinges broke loose from one side of the backboard. The backboard didn't fall, it just swung down, slamming into the wall and shattering glass everywhere!"

"Oh gosh!" Anne blurted. "Was anyone hurt?"

"Mostly cuts from the glass. But it was so loud. No one saw it dropping until it was too late. Then everyone screamed and jumped up. Susan looked like she was in pure shock. That backboard swung down right over her head! It missed her by inches!"

"Lucky thing she's so short," Anne said. "The coach said the blow would have killed her. I can't believe you didn't hear about it." Beth hopped up. "Anyway, I've got to go. Nicole and I are going to the mall. You want to come?"

Juniper took her place back on the couch. "She has other plans today."

Beth ignored her and continued looking at Anne for an answer.

"I can't go out," Anne said, pointing to her stitches.

"Ewwwww, that looks bad. Will you be at school tomorrow?"

"I think so," Anne said. "But I'll have to sit and watch during cheer practice."

"Toodles." Beth walked around Gena and headed out.

"Toodles," Gena said, mocking Beth once she was gone. "That must be the language they speak on the planet Snot."

Juniper giggled. "Yeah, she's the only thing that can gross me out more than Anne's injury."

Anne leaned back, ignoring their remarks. Her mind was rewinding. She closed her eyes and saw the truck rolling at her. She relived the panic. She felt every moment again in her mind.

Beth and Juniper were still talking. "I wish I could have seen that backboard shatter though," Gena said. "I bet that was awesome."

Juniper nodded. "It's a lucky thing Susan is such a shorty."

Anne bolted straight up. "Susan is the shortest cheerleader on the squad!"

"She's definitely a munchkin," Gena said.

"I'm the tallest."

The silence was deafening. Juniper and Gena both had a shocked look, the same look Anne figured she was wearing at that moment.

"Anne," Juniper said slowly. "If you'd been there . . ."

"You heard what Beth said." Anne shivered as the realism set in. "The blow would have killed her."

All three of them looked down at Anne's leg.

"That wreck saved your life, Anne," Juniper said.

Anne was stunned. She tried to breath normally, but her lungs felt tight and closed. With a trembling voice she said, "Guess there's something to this fate business after all." She picked up the Hand of Fate and rubbed it with her thumbs.

Gena shrugged. "Fate happens."

The doorbell rang again.

Mom barreled through, wiping her hands and smelling like egg salad. "This is a busy house today." She left the door partially opened. "Anne, someone for you." Mom hurried back to the kitchen with a grin.

Anne looked at Juniper and Gena. Who in the world was it this time? And why hadn't Mom invited the person in? She hobbled over and pulled back the door. There stood Troy Messina, holding a bouquet of wildflowers. He fidgeted back and forth, scratching his head, then neck, then arm.

"Hi."

Troy quickly held out the flowers. "I just came by to see if you were feeling better. Does your leg still hurt? Are you coming to school tomorrow?"

"I'll be at school." Anne figured answering the second question would answer the first one too. She accepted the flowers, although she worried about sending Troy the wrong message.

Troy stood with his hands tucked under his armpits. He looked around, avoiding Anne's eyes.

"Thanks for these," Anne said. She didn't invite him in. She couldn't deal with the teasing from Juniper and Gena.

Troy pivoted and started down the sidewalk. "See you at school," he called back over his shoulder.

"See you."

Anne closed the door and faced Juniper and Gena. They burst out laughing, as she had expected. "Can it!" she said, limping to the kitchen.

She reached up for a vase and filled it with water. Mom came over as Anne slipped the flowers inside.

"Those are lovely," she said.

Anne figured she was fishing. "That's the boy who was at the scene of the wreck. He was just concerned."

Mom nodded and walked away.

Anne placed the flowers on the kitchen table. Mom was right. Even though Troy had obviously picked them himself, they were lovely. She leaned over to smell them, letting the scent fill her. She suddenly realized the moment. How lucky she was to be here. Alive.

She looked out the window at a squirrel racing up and down a tree in her backyard. She soaked in the colors, the movement, everything. Then she was hit with another smell. Faint, but obvious. The scent of baby powder.

ABOUT DOTTI ENDERLE

Dotti Enderle is a Capricorn with E.S.P.—extra silly personality. She sleeps with the Three of Cups tarot card under her pillow to help her dream up new ideas for the Fortune Tellers Club. Dotti lives in Texas with her husband, two daughters, a cat, and a pesky ghost named Shakespeare. Learn more about Dotti and her books at:

www.fortunetellersclub.com

Here's a glimpse of what's ahead in Fortune Tellers Club #6,
Mirror, Mirror . . .

CHAPTER 1

Staring Back

Meow. Gena stirred in her sleep, dreaming of cotton candy sticking to her chin.

Meow.

More cotton candy. She just couldn't seem to keep it in her mouth. It grew wetter and stickier and . . . *Meow.*

She woke up to a pair of shiny mismatched eyes staring into hers. "Shhhh, Twilight!" she said, cuddling the cat close. "We'll get busted for sure."

The cat continued to lick her chin. "Okay, okay."

Meow.

"Shhhh!" She heard stirring in the next room. *Danger! Danger!* "Bye-bye, Twilight."

Carrying the cat to the window, she opened it and lightly dropped him to the ground. She watched as he stretched and moseyed off for the day. Quickly, she sprayed the room with the "Freshness of Mountain Air," then hid the air freshener in a drawer. Another night without getting caught. Great! She headed off to breakfast.

"You're up early again," her dad said as she entered the kitchen.

"Yeah. Well. You know." She walked around him to get the cereal from the pantry.

"It's just that you're not usually an early riser. Are you really my daughter, or is this one of those *Invasion of the Body Snatchers* scenarios?"

"Trust me, Dad, it's me. I only let the aliens take over while I'm bored in class."

He snickered as he poured another cup of coffee. "I'm off to work."

Gena looked at the clock. Wow, it *was* early, even for a school morning. She relaxed as she ate her breakfast, then went to the bathroom to brush her teeth. She wet the brush, squeezed on some toothpaste, and grinned toward the mirror. *What?* Her heart jumped a high hurdle, and she stumbled back, dropping the icky toothpaste off her brush. The reflection in the mirror wasn't hers.

She stared forward, taking a moment to catch her breath. Was she still asleep? That had to be it. She was never up this early anyway, so it must be a dream. She pinched herself hard. "Ouch!" *Okay, not a dream.* She inched forward and so did the reflection. Gena looked down at the green tee shirt she wore with the words *Girls Kick Butt* on the front. Peeking up, she saw that her reflection had been staring down at a neatly pressed white shirt. Gena touched the mirror. Who was this? For a moment she thought she'd faint.

She clamped her eyes shut, her heart pounding wildly. *I'm not crazy. I'm not crazy. Slowly opening her eyes—I'm not cra . . . uuuuuuuughhhhhhhh!*

The strange reflection still lingered. Long blond hair in braids, tiny nose, uni-brow. *Yuck! Buy some tweezers, girl!*

This was clearly not Gena, but the reflection moved as though it was—every single, teeny tiny maneuver.

There's a logical explanation. This is too freaky to be real. It's a trick! "Ah ha!" Gena shouted. She scrambled around, looking for a camera. "You don't fool me. This is really just a glass window, and I'm on one of those lame hidden camera shows. All right, where is it? And where's the microphone. Come on, I hate reality TV!"

Gena used her peripheral vision to watch as the reflection looked for the camera too. And the girls mouth moved with every word Gena spoke. "Not cool," Gena said, tapping on the glass.

She left the bathroom, walked back to her bedroom, and felt a ripple of shock when the girl occupied her dresser mirror too. "This is impossible. I look like one of the preppy girls at school, only with one eyebrow." Her heart still raced, but she was determined to stay calm.

Gena went into her dad's bedroom, his bathroom, and even found an old hand mirror to check herself out. All the same.

She wilted across her bed, shivering, afraid to look anymore. This had to be some sort of joke. No, the joke came when she looked at the alarm clock. 7:45. Great, only fifteen minutes to get dressed and off to school. She kept her back to the mirror and brushed her teeth. She stumbled out of the bathroom and managed to avoid the bedroom mirror too as she got dressed.

Even though she was alone in the house, she felt like that reflection, whoever she was, was watching her. She shuffled all her books and papers into her backpack and headed for the front door. Wait! Gena stamped her foot as she remembered that she hadn't brushed her hair. *So what else is new?* she thought, running her fingers through it. But the ends were plastered together from being too close to her chin while Twilight had given her a tongue bath. "Arrrrgh!" It had to be brushed.

I can do this without looking. She threw her hair up in a ponytail, but felt a cowlick sticking up near the side. She pulled out the elastic band and tried again.

"It would help if I could see what I was doing!" Gena hoped the reflection could hear that. Another cowlick. *Yuck!* She pulled the ponytail down and brushed her hair hard. This time it went up smoothly. As a natural reflex, she glanced toward the mirror. *Ick!* Maybe Dad was right. This must be a case of the Body Snatchers.

THE LOST GIRL

Fortune Tellers Club

DOTTI ENDERLE

Twelve-year-old Juniper and her friends Anne and Gena call themselves the Fortune Tellers Club. For the past two years they've helped each other using Ouija boards, tarot cards, crystals, and other forms of divination.

When Gena misplaces her retainer, she turns to her friends for help. After several dead-end clues using the Ouija board, Juniper (the truly psychic member of the club) tries crystal gazing using a bowl of water. But instead of locating the retainer, she sees the gaunt face of a young girl.

The image is that of a missing child, nine-year-old Laurie Simmons. Now, the Fortune Tellers Club will stop at nothing, natural or supernatural, to find her.

ISBN 0-7387-0253-6
144 pp., 5 3/16 x 7 5/8
$4.99

To order, call 1-877-NEW-WRLD
Prices subject to change without notice

Playing with Fire

Fortune Tellers Club

DOTTI ENDERLE

Can divination and magic help the girls solve this latest burning mystery?

The second installment of the Fortune Tellers Club series crackles with suspense! Anne Donovan has a crush on Eric, the new boy at school. No one knows much about him except that he transferred schools after his house went up in flames.

Anne and her two friends, who call themselves the Fortune Tellers Club, spread the tarot cards to predict Anne's future as Eric's girlfriend. When a series of fires breaks out, including one that destroys the school library, their attention turns to a more burning question. Does Eric possesses a special power—pyrokinesis? They set to work searching for answers before everything around them turns to cinders.

ISBN 0-7387-0340-0
160 pp., 5³⁄₁₆ x 7⁵⁄₈
$4.99

To order, call 1-877-NEW-WRLD
Prices subject to change without notice

THE MAGIC SHADES

Fortune Tellers Club

DOTTI ENDERLE

Can Gena trust what she sees through those fifty-cent sunglasses? While rummaging through a resale shop, wisecracking tomboy Gena finds an enticing pair of mirrored cat-eye sunglasses.

Anne and Juniper, Gena's best friends and fellow members of the Fortune Tellers Club, don't exactly share Gena's enthusiasm for her new shades. They like them even less when they discover they are windows to the future, through which Gena can see things like the answers to her science test.

Are the glasses a blessing or a curse? When they show her dad's new girlfriend snooping in Gena's bedroom and her dad lying in a pool of blood in the kitchen, Gena's life takes an interesting turn.

ISBN 0-7387-0341-9
144 pp., 5³⁄₁₆ x 7⁵⁄₈
$4.99

To order, call 1-877-NEW-WRLD
Prices subject to change without notice